For Tori and Liam - PK
For Tilly - CC

First published in Great Britain 2016 by Egmont UK Limited
This edition published 2019 by Dean,
an imprint of Egmont UK Limited,
The Yellow Building, 1 Nicholas Road, London W11 4AN

www.egmont.co.uk

Text copyright © Paddy Kempshall 2016
Illustrations copyright © Egmont UK Limited 2016

The moral rights of the author have been asserted.

ISBN 978 0 6035 7759 8
70742/001
Printed in Malaysia

A CIP catalogue record for this title is available from the British Library.

Stay safe online.
Egmont is not responsible for content hosted by third parties.

Egmont takes its responsibility to the planet and its inhabitants very seriously.
We aim to use papers from well-managed forests run by responsible suppliers.

PETE'S MAGIC PANTS

THE LOST DINOSAUR

PADDY KEMPSHALL • CHRIS CHATTERTON

DEAN

In a wobbly old wardrobe, in the attic of Crooked Carrot Farm, a special suitcase lay hidden for many years …

Until Pete found it one day and discovered something wonderfully weird – the suitcase was packed with amazing MAGIC PANTS!

There were big ones, baggy ones,
hairy ones and scary ones; fluffy ones,
singing ones and even some with ears –
but that's another story!

Each pair didn't just look awesome – they could also whisk Pete off on the most amazing adventures whenever he popped them on!

Pants Away!"

"Cool!" said Pete, wriggling into the hairiest pants you ever did see. "Caveman pants! I wonder if I'll meet a dinosaur . . .

And the hairy pants started to
wiggle,
wobble,

shimmy
and **shake**.

Then, with a twangy ping, Pete found himself
slowly spinning on top of an egg!

As he came to a stop, he noticed
a small chicken carrying a big club
and a blue skateboard.

"Uh-oh," clucked the chicken,
"you in trouble now. You better get
off that egg before it . . .

CRACKS!"

Out popped a baby dinosaur
and licked Pete on the nose!

"Dada?" said the dinosaur.

"I'm not your daddy, but
I'm sure I can find him," said Pete.

The small chicken tapped Pete on the arm
and puffed out his chest. "Me, Ted. Me good
dinosaur finder. Will help find Dino Dada."

So Pete and the baby dinosaur followed Ted through the dark forest as he snuffled and sniffed the leaves.

Eventually, Ted stopped and pointed at a large tree. "Me found Dino Dada," he beamed. "Him behind there."

Suddenly there was a loud rumble and the tree shook as
an enormous T. rex with HUGE TEETH crashed through the branches.

"Um . . . I don't think that's the Dino Dada . . ." gulped Pete,
"but I do think it's hungry! Run!"

Sweeping up the baby dinosaur,
Pete leapt onto Ted's skateboard.
"Skate for your life, Ted!" he called.

"Him . . . PUFF . . . too . . .
PANT . . . fast!" gasped Ted,
as the ferocious T. rex
SNAP-SNAP-SNAPPED
behind them.

"Just keep going!" yelled Pete, grabbing a bendy branch and heaving it back, until . . .

TWAAAANG!

"He no catch us now,"
clucked Ted.

"No," gulped Pete, goggling at the gang of hungry dinosaurs pouring out of the bushes. "But those Velociraptors might! Come on!"

Whizzing through the forest,
Pete steered the skateboard
past flashing fangs
and sharp claws.

He swerved in and out
of twisty trees . . .

whizzed up and
down huge hills . . .

and raced round
rubbly rocks.

"I think we've lost them," puffed Pete,
"and I know how to find the Dino Dada!"

They climbed up a very tall tree and looked out across
the land. And what a spectacular sight lay before them.

There were lots of dinosaurs – including a very large
one with purple spots, just like the baby dinosaur.

"There!" cried Pete. "That's the Dino Dada we're looking for!
We need to go through the swamp."

Squelching and squishing through the smelly
swamp, Pete and his friends searched for hours,
but the Dino Dada was nowhere to be seen.

"I don't understand," sighed Pete, slumping down
beside a huge tree trunk. "He should be somewhere near this tree."

Ted cleared his throat. "That no tree," he clucked. "That dino leg!"

"Dada!" squeaked the baby dinosaur.

"My son!" boomed the enormous dinosaur. "You've found him. And I know just how to say thank you!"

The Dino Dada bent his neck and Pete, Ted and the baby dinosaur climbed up onto his back. Ever so slowly, he plodded out of the forest . . .

And took them on an amazing dinosaur safari!
Pete couldn't believe how many different
types of dinosaur there were.
"Best . . . day . . . ever!"
he shouted.

"Three cheers for Pete. Him best dinosaur finder in land," cried Ted.

But finally it was time to go.

and **shimmy**
from his magic pants . . .

Then with a
shake

Pete was back in the attic once more.

"Wow," cheered Pete,

"that was **dino-tastic!**"